THE CASE OF
THE PLANETARIUM
PUZZLE

Written by Vivian Binnamin
Illustrated by Jeffrey S. Nelsen

Silver Press

Library of Congress Cataloging-in-Publication Data

Library of Congress Cataloging-in-Publication Data
Binnamin, Vivian.
    The case of the planetarium puzzle / by Vivian
Binnamin; illustrations by Jeffrey S. Nelsen.
        p.   cm.—(Field trip mysteries)
    Summary: The Fantastic Fifteen solve the puzzle of the
strange salad the planetarium teacher has left for them.
    [1. Mystery and detective stories.   2. Planets—
Fiction.]   I. Nelsen, Jeffrey S, ill.   II. Title.   III. Series:
Binnamin, Vivian. Field trip mysteries.
PZ7.B51183Catm   1989   [E]—dc20   89-39378
CIP   AC
ISBN 0-671-68823-5 (pbk.)
ISBN 0-671-68819-7 (lib. bdg.)

Published by Silver Press, a division of
Silver Burdett Press, Inc.,
Simon & Schuster, Inc.,
Prentice Hall Bldg., Englewood Cliffs, NJ 07632.
Printed in the United States of America.

10 9 8 7 6 5 4 3 2 1

Attention All Detectives!

Yes, you can be a detective, too,
right along with Miss Whimsy
and the Fantastic Fifteen. Just
pay close attention to the story
and the pictures in the book.
There are clues hidden there,
and the Fantastic Fifteen will
be looking for them. See if you
can discover them first!

Our teacher, Miss Whimsy, calls us the Fantastic Fifteen. And for good reason!

Miss Whimsy taught us to peek, poke, and prove. That's right. She solves mysteries. Miss Whimsy is a great detective. Now we're great detectives, too. That is a good thing, because wherever we go, mysteries seem to follow.

Miss Whimsy's
Third Grade

the

Fantastic
Fifteen

"Can you name the planets?" asked Miss Whimsy. "Knowing them may help you peek, poke, and prove at the City Planetarium today."

Can you put the planets in the right order?

Mercury Venus Earth Mars

Jupiter

Sun

Saturn

Uranus Neptune

Pluto

Yesterday we pretended to be the planets. Miss Whimsy took us to the park behind school. Dee was the Sun. Zoe was Mercury. Eve was Venus. Kelvin was Earth. Tom was Mars. Kelly, Naoto, Simon, Casey, and Bo were Jupiter, Saturn, Uranus, Neptune, and Pluto.

"Here's the Sun," said Miss Whimsy, moving Dee out on the grass. "All right, planets, find your places."

We fanned out around Dee, the Sun. "Now you'll always remember the order of the planets," said Miss Whimsy.

The City Planetarium is just up the street. So we got to walk to our field trip!

Inside, the planetarium room was round and filled with seats. The ceiling had a high dome. Something very strange was in the middle. It looked like a creature from outer space.

"It's a planetarium projector," explained Miss Whimsy. "It shines pictures of the night sky on the ceiling dome."

The room was quiet and empty.

"Very strange," said Miss Whimsy. "Where could Miss Luna be?"

Then Tom looked behind the door. He found a note. Miss Whimsy read:

 City Planetarium

Dear Miss Whimsy,
Sorry I had to leave.
Directions are on the control
desk. Take my place, Miss
Whimsy. You can do it!

Best wishes,
Miss Luna
Planetarium
Teacher.

Miss Whimsy took a deep breath. Then she stepped behind the control desk. It was covered with dials and buttons — just like a rocket ship.

Directions:

Miss Whimsy pressed buttons and turned dials on the control panel. At first nothing happened. Then the lights went out. The dome filled with stars.

"Wow!" said the Fantastic Fifteen.

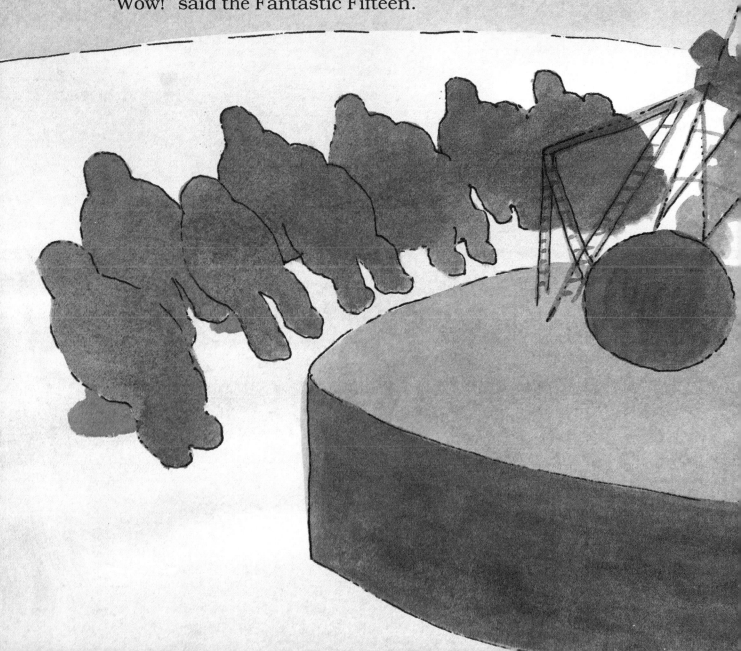

"First we'll see stars and constellations," said Miss Whimsy. "Constellations are groups of stars."

We saw the Great Bear, the Little Dog, and Leo the Lion in the sky. We saw the North Star, the Little Dipper, and the Big Dipper.

We saw asteroids, meteors, and comets. We saw all the planets...from Mercury to Pluto.

When the lights came on, Miss Whimsy looked behind the desk.
She pulled out a brown paper bag with letters on it. Miss Whimsy read
aloud.

To Miss Whimsy
and the Fantastic
Fifteen:

I hear you are great detectives.
Can you solve the mystery of this
strange salad? What does it mean?
Leave the solution for me. And,
don't eat the evidence.
         Good Luck!
                    Miss Luna
                    Planetarium Teacher

Miss Whimsy peeked inside the bag. Then she slowly turned it upside down. Out tumbled two sesame seeds, a peppercorn, two peas, a red apple, a lemon, and two grapes.

We had our mystery . . . and it was not an easy one. But we were tough. And we were ready for the case of the planetarium puzzle.

"Peek!" said Miss Whimsy with a wink. "Time to look for clues."

We peeked around and around the planetarium. We saw rockets. We saw space shuttles. We saw star charts and planet maps. We saw earth globes and moon models.

PLANET FACTS

1. Of all the planets, Venus has the longest day.
2. Mercury and Venus have no moons!

SPACE SHUTTLE

"Time to poke!" said Miss Whimsy.

Bo and Kelvin found a picture of a famous comet. A comet is probably just a dirty snowball traveling through space. But it sure looks like more than that!

HALLEY'S COMET
Halley's Comet reappears every 76-79 years.

Eve, Zoe, and Tom found a strange rock. Only it turned out not to be an earth rock at all.

METEORITE

Meteors are sometimes called shooting stars. Made of metal or stone, they glow as they fly through the earth's atmosphere. If they hit the earth, they are called Meteorites.

"Look! The planets!" said Dee.
We looked at a model of the solar system.
Each of us studied the planet we had pretended to be.

We poked and poked. By the time Miss Whimsy whistled, we had it.

"We did it," said Zoe. "We solved the case of the planetarium puzzle."
"Prove it," said Miss Whimsy.
"Miss Luna left us two sesame seeds, a peppercorn, two peas, an apple, a lemon, and two grapes," said Kelvin. "Nine things!"

"Remember when we pretended to be the nine planets?" asked Dee.

"One thing was wrong," said Casey.

"We're all about the same size," said Zoe. "But the planets aren't."

"Watch," said Bo.

Zoe placed the two sesame seeds, the peppercorn, two peas, the apple, the lemon, and the two grapes on big white paper on the floor. She wrote on the paper. Then she wrote a note on the brown bag.

Miss Whimsy looked
and smiled.
"Ah, yes!" she said.
"Again, you've proved
you're the Fantastic
Fifteen. Leave everything
as it is. Miss Luna will
be more than pleased."

And that is just what we did. When she returned, this is what Miss Luna saw:

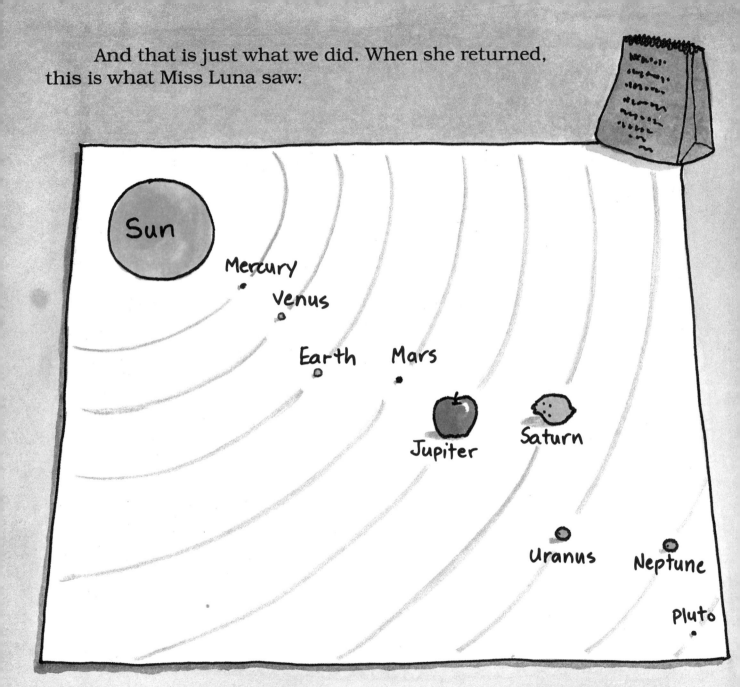

Did you solve the planetarium puzzle with the Fantastic Fifteen?